SPIDER-

THE NEW GOBLIN

MW00748651

COLUMBIA PICTURES PRESENTS A MARVEL STUDIOS/LAURA ZISKIN PRODUCTION A SAM RAIMI FILM TOBEY MAGUIRE 'SPIDER-MAN 3' KIRSTEN DUNST JAMES FRANCO THOMAS HADEN CHURCH TOPHER GRACE BRYCE DALLAS HOWARD MUSIC BY DANNY ELFMAN SCORE CHRISTOPHER YOUNG EXECUTIVE PRODUCERS STAN LEE KEVIN FEIGE JOSEPH M. CARACCIOLO BASED ON THE MARVEL COMIC BOOK BY STAN LEE AND STEVE DITKO

MARVEL SPIDER-MAN CHARACTER TM & © 2006 MARVEL CHARACTERS, INC. ALL RIGHTS RESERVED.   SCREEN STORY BY SAM RAIMI & IVAN RAIMI SCREENPLAY BY ALVIN SARGENT PRODUCED BY LAURA ZISKIN AVI ARAD GRANT CURTIS DIRECTED BY SAM RAIMI   COLUMBIA PICTURES

sony.com/Spider-Man

Spider-Man and all related characters: ™ & © 2007 Marvel Characters, Inc.
Spider-Man 3, the movie: © 2007 Columbia Pictures Industries, Inc.
All Rights Reserved.
HarperCollins®, ☰®, and HarperEntertainment™
are trademarks of HarperCollins Publishers.

Spider-Man 3: The New Goblin
Printed in the United States of America.
All rights reserved.
No part of this book may be used or reproduced in any manner whatsoever
without written permission except in the case of brief quotations
embodied in critical articles and reviews.
For information address HarperCollins Children's Books,
a division of HarperCollins Publishers,
1350 Avenue of the Americas, New York, NY 10019.
www.harpercollinschildrens.com

Library of Congress catalog card number: 2006934363
ISBN-10: 0-06-083724-1 — ISBN-13: 978-0-06-083724-2

Book design by John Sazaklis

❖

SPIDER-MAN 3
THE NEW GOBLIN™

By Danny Fingeroth

Screenplay by Alvin Sargent

Screen Story by Sam Raimi & Ivan Raimi

Based on the Marvel Comic Book by Stan Lee and Steve Ditko

HarperEntertainment
An Imprint of HarperCollinsPublishers

CHAPTER
7

The room was dark except for the shaft of moonlight shining through the open terrace door. The wind blowing in whispered through the silk curtains. Harry Osborn looked around and saw movement in the corner, and then he saw himself reflected in large black eyes.

Spider-Man had Harry's father, Norman, cornered. The masked menace crouched, ready to spring.

"I'm going to kill you, Norman," the wall-crawler hissed. "Nothing can save you."

Harry couldn't let this happen! He had to save his father! He tried to scream for Spider-Man to stop, but no words came out of his mouth.

His father turned and looked at him. "Save me, Harry!" Norman pleaded. "For once in your life, do something!"

"I'm trying, Dad," said Harry, finally able to speak. "I'm trying!" He lunged forward, but he couldn't get any closer to them. His legs felt frozen. His father was going to die—and there was nothing Harry could do to stop it!

Spider-Man laughed underneath his mask. Harry suddenly noticed that Spider-Man grasped a jagged, pointed metal spike in his hands.

Harry stretched his arms out in front of him until his shoulders felt like they would pop out of their sockets, but he still couldn't reach the two men. Why couldn't he do anything? Why?

Spider-Man reared back and hurled the spike. It found its mark, and, in seconds, Norman Osborn was dead.

Spider-Man's laughter echoed through the mansion. Then the laughter turned to screams— Harry's own screams!

Harry jerked up in bed, drenched in sweat. The nightmare had seemed so real . . . but that's all it had been: a nightmare.

Even though it was just a dream, and he hadn't actually seen his father die, Harry was certain Spider-Man had killed him. After all, it was Spider-Man who had brought his father's body home that terrible night, and then ran away. No one else could be responsible.

Harry had recently made two discoveries that convinced him even more that Spider-Man was his father's murderer. Each discovery was shocking on its own. Together, they turned his life upside down.

The first discovery was about Spider-Man himself. Harry had found out that Spider-Man was really Harry's former best friend, Peter Parker! It made Harry sick, the way his father's killer had pretended to be his friend.

The other discovery was equally distressing, and was connected to the first. Harry had found—in the very Manhattan mansion in which he now slept—a secret room that had belonged to his father. In that room were all the weapons, gadgets, and devices that had belonged to the supervillain known as the Green Goblin.

Examining the notes and other papers in the secret room left no doubt about why the villain's things were in the Osborn mansion. Harry had to face the fact that Norman Osborn had been the Green Goblin!

Spider-Man and the Green Goblin were enemies. They had battled violently all over New York City. So it made sense that Spider-Man—*Peter!*—had killed his father in battle. But it was too much for Harry to deal with.

If his father was the Green Goblin—then his father was evil. Maybe he'd attacked Spider-Man first. But even if that were true, what kind of a son would Harry be if he let his father's killer walk the streets? He had to do something, but what? He imagined the response he'd get if he walked into a police station and said: "Excuse me, officer. My name is Harry Osborn. My father was the Green Goblin, and I have reason to believe my best friend—who happens to be Spider-Man— killed him." They'd think he was insane!

His head filled with conflicting thoughts, Harry roamed the dark mansion until he found himself facing the full-length mirror that hid the secret entrance to his father's goblin lair. But when he looked in the mirror, he didn't see his own reflection. He saw something impossible.

The face of Norman Osborn stared back at him from the mirror. Harry rubbed his eyes, but Norman's face didn't waver. He knew the look on his father's face well. It was the look he had always given Harry when he was disappointed in him—which had been pretty often. Norman was a hard man to please. Ironically, Norman had always been impressed with *Peter's* abilities in science and often praised *him*. Harry sometimes thought Norman would have preferred having Peter as his son.

Now Harry could hear Norman's voice taunting him. "Spider-Man killed me, Harry. You know who he is. You know where he lives. Yet you do nothing to avenge my death."

Harry rubbed his eyes again. When he

looked in the mirror this time, all he saw was his own tired face. His shoulders sagged in relief. But he knew Norman would be back. Alive or dead, his father knew just how to make Harry's life miserable.

CHAPTER
2

Peter Parker had never been happier. As he walked through Times Square, he thought about how his life had changed. A few years ago, Peter had been bitten by a genetically altered spider while visiting a museum exhibit, and that bite had given him the powers of the spider. He could climb walls, spin webs, and move very fast, and he had great strength. He used these powers to fight crime as Spider-Man. The only people who knew that Peter was Spider-Man were Peter's girlfriend, Mary Jane Watson, and his best friend, Harry Osborn.

Spider-Man had done a lot of good for New York City, defeating the Green Goblin and Doctor Octopus, as well as other, lesser-known criminals. To show its thanks, the city planned to honor him officially with a special ceremony.

Walking down Broadway, he saw the stage

being set up for the ceremony. The next day Spider-Man was to be given the key to the city. It wasn't a real key, of course—it wouldn't open anything—but it showed how much everyone liked Spider-Man and how happy they were to have him around. The key to the city meant that he was accepted. For a guy like Peter, who'd grown up being called "bookworm" and "nerd," that acceptance meant a lot.

Peter finally reached his destination: a Broadway theater. On its marquee, big letters announced that a play called *Manhattan Memories* was running and that one of its stars was Mary Jane Watson. There was a big photo of a smiling M.J. on the front of the theater.

Inside the theater, Peter took the front-row-center seat that she had saved for him. The lights went down and the curtain rose. On stage, M.J. was bathed in a bright spotlight and sang in a soft but lovely voice. *"They say that falling in love is wonderful, it's wonderful . . ."* It seemed as if she were singing just for him.

In the last row of the balcony, Harry Osborn was also watching the show. Through his opera glasses, he saw Peter in the first row and Mary Jane singing to him. Harry could have easily afforded any seat in the theater, but he didn't want to deal with Peter and Mary Jane directly, so he had gotten a seat far away from the stage. Mary Jane had once been Harry's girlfriend, before she started dating Peter. Their happiness gave Harry one more reason to resent Peter.

When the show was over, Harry quickly made his way out of the theater, hoping to leave without being noticed. But Peter saw him heading toward Harry's waiting limousine, and ran to catch up to his friend.

"Harry," Peter begged, "you've got to stop avoiding me. You need to stop locking me out. You need to hear the truth!"

Harry hesitated. But as he looked at the window of the car door, he saw Norman's reflection. "Don't weaken," said the reflection.

"I'm your friend, Harry," continued Peter.

"Your *father* was my friend."

Harry turned, and his eyes met Peter's. For a second, it seemed as if Harry might finally be willing to hear Peter's side of things. But again Harry heard Norman's voice in his head: "Don't weaken."

Harry's anger and confusion over his father's death returned. He got into the limo and slammed the door shut. The sound of the lock clicking into place echoed in Peter's ears. The limo took off and sped down the street.

What Harry didn't know was how Norman Osborn had *really* died.

It had happened in an abandoned building below the Queensboro Bridge. The Green Goblin and Spider-Man had been in a heated battle. Spider-Man was winning, but the Green Goblin had one sneaky trick left. Remotely controlling his spear-tipped glider, he sent it streaking toward Spider-Man's back. When Spider-Man realized what was happening, he leaped out of the way. The zooming glider missed him—and hit the Green Goblin, killing him. Norman Osborn's death had been his own doing!

Norman's dying request to Peter was that he not tell Harry his father had been the Green Goblin. So Peter removed the Goblin armor from Norman's body and, as Spider-Man, returned him to his son. In Harry's anger and sadness over his father's death, he had come to blame Spider-Man for it. And to honor Norman's wishes, Peter couldn't tell Harry what had really happened. Although Peter tried to talk to Harry about it, Harry didn't want to listen. He wasn't ready to forgive or to forget.

CHAPTER
3

Harry paced the floor of the mansion's great room, lost in troubled thoughts. His loyal butler, Bernard, looked in on him and shook his head. He was worried about Harry, but Bernard knew better than to try and talk to him when he was so upset.

I should have spoken to Peter, thought Harry. *He was my best friend. I should give him a chance to explain, shouldn't I? But he killed my father—how can I ever forgive that? But maybe I should have him over . . . try to talk things out . . .*

Once again, Harry heard the voice of his father echoing inside his head.

"You have the power to pay him back!" said Norman. "Use it!"

"I do?" said Harry. "He has all those spider-powers. I'm nowhere near his level."

"Don't pretend you don't know what I'm talking about," sneered Norman's voice.

Harry did know. And he knew that he'd never be able to make a decision about Peter until he had power of his own. Harry had seen the Green Goblin's secret lab and the racks of goblin armor and weapons. He had read and reread his father's notebooks and diaries. He didn't have the power yet—but it was waiting for him in the hidden room.

Harry stood up straight and tall. He walked to the mirrored door and pressed the hidden latch. The door slid open and revealed the goblin lair inside. A hissing sound filled the lab. It came from the shimmering green gas that swirled inside a brightly lit glass chamber. The green glow from the gas gave a weird tint to everything in the room—including Harry.

Harry walked past the hanging suits of goblin armor, goblin masks, pumpkin bombs, razor-edged throwing-bats, and the rest of the Green

Goblin's arsenal. He opened the door to the chamber and, without pausing, stepped inside. He closed the door behind him.

The swirling green gas felt like acid on Harry's skin. He screamed in pain. But within seconds, the pain was replaced by a feeling of great power. Harry was changing. Every cell of his body felt charged with more energy than he had ever imagined.

Then, all at once, the gas cleared and the chamber door swung open. Harry stepped out. Now he understood the power that the Green Goblin had had at his fingertips. And now he felt the rage of the Green Goblin. Everything suddenly became clear to him. He had no need to fear Peter anymore. Harry was strong, too—and now he was determined. He had one mission: destroy Peter Parker.

Harry reached for a suit of armor. He put it on and then looked at himself in the mirror. But he did not see his own reflection.

He saw the proud, laughing face of Norman Osborn.

CHAPTER 4

Harry soared across the Manhattan sky on
the goblin Sky-Stick. It took a little while to
get used to traveling this way, but Harry was
getting the hang of it. What a view of the city he
had! The people below seemed like ants he could
crush at will.

There was only one insect he was concerned
about right now: Spider-Man. Harry had let his
feelings for Peter and Mary Jane allow him to be
weak. No more. He had power now. He had the
armor, too. In his dream he wasn't able to do anything to punish his father's killer. Now, in real life,
there was nothing to stop him.

Harry landed the Sky-Stick on a rooftop across
the street from the *Daily Bugle* building. He
waited. Before long, he heard the sound of a
familiar motorbike as it roared down the block.

Unseen, Harry tailed the motorbike through the city. When the bike came to a stop, the driver removed his helmet, revealing the smiling face of Peter Parker. As Peter got off the bike and started toward his apartment building's front door, he suddenly felt an intense tingling in the back of his head. It was his Spidey sense! Peter leaped out of the way—but the attack came too fast for him to avoid. The jet-powered Sky-Stick, piloted by the masked and armored Harry, hit him full force, pulling him from the street and up into the sky.

As Peter struggled to get free, a pair of nasty-looking blades popped out of this New Goblin's wrist armor. He swung them at Peter, slicing his chest! Peter screamed in pain.

As the New Goblin prepared to strike again, Peter used his spider-strength to kick himself away, and then flip up and over the New Goblin's head. Peter was free—but falling toward the pavement, many stories below! Harry watched his "friend" fall—and did nothing to save him—just as no one had done anything to save his father!

But Peter was far from helpless. He shot a web-line from his wrist toward a nearby building ledge. Harry realized that Peter was going to use the line to stop his fall and swing away. Before Peter could do either, the Sky-Stick swooped in and the New Goblin tore the web-line in two with his wrist blades! Peter kept falling—until he was slammed again by the Sky-Stick! The assault sent him shooting into the side of a building, and he found himself embedded in the brick wall by the force of the impact!

Peter still didn't know who this New Goblin was, but as the Sky-Stick came to a hover in front of Peter, Harry slid his mask back to reveal his face. It gave Harry great pleasure that Peter now knew the identity of the one who would kill him.

"Face it, Pete," he said. "It had to come to this."

Harry swung at Peter with the wrist armor again. But Peter tore himself from the wall just in time, so that Harry's blades cut only into the bricks. Peter landed nearby, sticking to the wall with his amazing power to adhere to any surface.

"I didn't kill your father, Harry. What you saw isn't what it seemed."

"SHUT UP!" screamed Harry, as he tore away the section of wall Peter was perched on. Harry had become as powerful as his father—if not *more* powerful! He kept coming at Peter, throwing chunks of wall at him, as well as pumpkin bombs and razor-edged throwing-bats. It was only a matter of time before he'd finish off his father's killer for good!

Shooting a web-line, Peter swung down to a narrow, winding alley. *I've got him on the run now,* thought Harry. *He's desperate to escape. This is fun!*

Firing web-line after web-line, Peter swung as fast as he could through the alley, throwing everything in his path back at Harry.

"Pathetic, Parker!" Harry shouted at him, as he nimbly piloted the Sky-Stick above and around the garbage cans, old tires, discarded furniture, and other junk that Peter hurled at him. He was zooming closer and closer to his prey.

Peter swung and climbed to a high point on a wall, and then spun around a corner. Harry laughed with glee as he prepared for the big finish. His father would be so proud of him! The high-and-mighty Spider-Man was reduced to fleeing like a scared mouse—by the New Goblin!

Harry zoomed around the corner at ninety miles per hour. He saw Peter just yards ahead of him, cornered, with nowhere to run.

Suddenly, the Sky-Stick hit something Harry couldn't see! Peter had shot a web-line directly in Harry's path just before he had rounded the corner. Harry flew off the Sky-Stick and hurtled toward the ground below. He hit the pavement with a loud thud.

Everything went black.

CHAPTER

5

Harry woke up in a hospital bed. He wasn't sure how he'd ended up there. He knew there had been some kind of accident, but he couldn't remember what had happened. He just knew that he was lucky to be alive. The doctors told him he could go home soon, but he couldn't picture where home was.

His thoughts were interrupted by people talking outside his room.

"How is he, doctor?" someone was asking. The voice seemed familiar, but who was it?

"Are you a relative?" the doctor asked.

"I'm his . . . best friend," the voice replied. Now Harry recognized it. *Peter!* Man, was he glad Peter was here!

"Is Harry going to be okay?" a woman's voice asked. *Mary Jane*, thought Harry. *She came, too!*

"He seems fine physically," said the doctor. "But . . ."

"But what?" Peter asked.

"He seems to be suffering from memory loss. He remembers his name . . . but everything else seems hazy."

That's for sure, thought Harry.

"Can we see him?" asked Mary Jane.

"Only for a minute," the doctor replied.

"Maybe we should just leave, M.J.," said Peter. "I've got to be the last person Harry wants to see right now."

That's strange, thought Harry. *Why would Peter think that? Did we have a fight or something?*

"You're going to have to face him sooner or later," said M.J. "Let's go inside."

As they entered his room, Harry recognized them—and he knew they were his friends. But beyond that, he couldn't remember anything else about them.

"Hiya, Harry," said Peter, smiling nervously.

"Pete! M.J.! It's so great to see you," whispered

Harry, still weak from his ordeal.

"It . . . it is?" said Peter.

"Of course it is," said Harry, smiling weakly. "It's times like this when you know who your friends really are." He grasped Peter's hand warmly with both of his.

"I'm sorry, but I have to ask you to leave," said an entering nurse. "Mr. Osborn needs to rest."

"Of course," said Peter.

As he and M.J. left the room, Harry drifted off to sleep. "My best friends," he said softly. "I'd . . . give my . . . life for them." His face clouded a little as one last thought crossed his mind before he fell asleep. "My father . . . ," he mumbled. "I think he died. . . ."

"Welcome home, Harry," said Bernard the butler. "Thank heaven you're all right."

"It's great to *be* home, Bernard," replied Harry, "although I hardly even remember this place."

Peter had brought Harry back from the hospital.

"It'll all come back to you, Harry," he said.

As Bernard headed upstairs with Harry's suitcase, Peter handed his friend a gift-wrapped box. "A homecoming present," he said. Harry smiled and eagerly removed the wrapping. Inside was an old basketball with the word PARKER written on it.

"Your old ball," Harry said. "I remember this. Thanks, buddy." Harry started dribbling the ball around the mansion's giant hallway. "We were pretty good in the backyard, weren't we?"

"We were *terrible*." Peter laughed.

Harry bounced the ball over to Peter, who caught it and tossed it back. "Looks like I'm not hurting for money," said Harry.

"You're *loaded*," Peter reminded him.

As they tossed the ball around, Harry and Peter passed a painted portrait of Norman Osborn. Peter held on to the ball as he and Harry looked up at the painting. "I think he always appreciated how you helped me get through high school, Peter. I wish I could remember more about him. . . ."

"He loved you, Harry," said Peter. "That's the main thing." Peter bounced the ball toward him. But Harry, lost in thought, didn't catch it. The ball bounded past him and crashed straight into a thin stand, upon which rested a priceless ancient vase.

The sound of the impact snapped Harry out of his thoughts. Faster than any normal person could, he steadied the wobbling stand *and* grabbed the falling vase before it could hit the floor.

"That's so weird," he said. "If we were terrible— how am I able to do something like that? And I have to tell you, Pete—I feel so strong, like I could do anything. And that doesn't seem familiar at all."

"Must be that hospital food," said Peter. "It works wonders."

"Yeah—that's it," replied Harry. "Man, I hope my memory comes back soon."

"Uh . . . me, too," said Peter.

Above them, the portrait of Norman Osborn seemed to be smiling.

CHAPTER
6

Spider-Man Day in New York was sunny and warm. The city was in the mood for a party. Banners and balloons proclaiming NY ❤S SPIDER-MAN! were everywhere. Children were running around in homemade Spider-Man costumes, imitating their hero. A large crowd was waiting for the key-awarding ceremony to begin. The mayor was making—or *trying* to make—a speech. But the chanting of the crowd drowned him out.

"SPIDER-MAN! SPIDER-MAN! SPIDER-MAN!"

Mary Jane was among the thousands of people eagerly awaiting Spider-Man's appearance. She was so proud of Peter.

"Hey, M.J.!" a voice called.

"Harry!" she said. She was glad to see a familiar face. But she was also concerned about what would happen if Harry's memory were to return fully.

"Where's Pete?" he asked.

"Taking somebody's picture, I guess," she replied evasively. Harry obviously didn't remember that his friend Peter *was* Spider-Man. "I'm so happy to see you, Harry. You look so good." The only sign of Harry's battle with Peter was a small bandage on his forehead.

"I never felt so good," said Harry. "It's a strange feeling, not knowing exactly who you are. You should try it sometime."

Up on the podium, a young blonde woman named Gwen Stacy was now speaking. She held a giant gold key in her hands. "We're all here to honor Spider-Man today," she said, "to thank him for all the good he's done. But I owe him a special thanks. Just the other day, he saved my life!" A runaway crane had put many people in danger until Spider-Man had come to the rescue, and Gwen had been one of the ones saved.

"So let's hear it," she shouted, "for the one, the only, the fabulous . . . Spider-Man!" On cue, the man of the hour swung down from a rooftop. Showing off for the crowd, he did some spins and somer-saults in the air. Finally, he lowered himself down on a web-line, upside down, to receive his award.

As Spider-Man took the key from her hands, Gwen impulsively reached up and pulled his mask off his chin. Then she leaned forward and kissed him full on the lips. The crowd went wild!

Mary Jane saw it and felt hurt and angry. *That's* our *special kiss*, she thought.

"I hope Pete's getting a shot of this!" said Harry, still not remembering who was under the mask.

"Let's get out of here," Mary Jane said.

"Sure, M.J.," Harry replied, noticing she seemed upset. "Hey, how about some ice cream? I seem to remember that's something that cheers people up!"

Away from the crowd, they found a small, gourmet ice cream parlor. Harry bought them both deluxe cones.

"You know . . . seeing you like this, M.J.," he said, ". . . it's suddenly bringing a memory back." That made Mary Jane nervous. What exactly would Harry remember?

"It's a little embarrassing," he continued, "but back in high school, I actually wrote a play for you. Never had the nerve to show it to you, though."

She was relieved that was all he remembered.

"I'd love to see it," she said.

"I think I have all my high school stuff in a box in my closet," Harry said. "Why don't you come over later for dinner? I'll dig it out. Maybe Peter can join us."

M.J. looked away for a moment before forcing a smile at Harry.

"Yeah, that'd be great," she said.

CHAPTER

7

That night, Harry was surprised by how excited he was to see Mary Jane again. When Bernard announced her arrival, Harry's heart gave a flutter. She looked a little sad, but she was more beautiful than ever. They hugged each other hello, and Harry held on for a few seconds.

"Where's Pete?" asked Harry.

"He, uh, couldn't make it," she replied. A brief look of annoyance flashed across her face, but then she smiled. "I'm ready for the play reading," she said.

"I thought we might have some dinner first," said Harry.

"Oh, if I'd known we were going out, I'd have dressed up," said Mary Jane.

"We're staying right here," said Harry, leading her to the kitchen. "And I'm cooking." She was touched. Mary Jane couldn't remember the last time Peter had made her a meal. He was always too busy studying or saving the world as Spider-Man.

While she chopped vegetables for a salad, Harry whipped up omelets for their dinner. He put some classic rock music on, and they danced as they cooked. The meal was delicious—and fun. Harry started to remember some of their relationship together. There were some wonderful memories of evenings out . . . and this evening was going so well, he began to feel that maybe there was a chance the two of them could get back together. He loved her so much. . . .

Finally, when dinner was over, Harry took out his old school notebook as they sat at the dining table.

"Be kind," he said. "It's real corny. I was in eleventh grade."

"I'll keep that in mind," laughed Mary Jane. "So, start reading."

"I wrote it for you," said Harry. "*You* read it."

Mary Jane cleared her throat and began reading her character's dialogue.

"'I've been everywhere, Richard. India, Africa, Greece. What's wrong with dreaming? Nothing like a little self deception to get you through the night.'"

"Oh, man," said Harry, groaning. "Did *I* write that?"

"It's beautiful," said Mary Jane. She looked at him warmly, touched that he had written that for her. Their faces were close to each other, and before either of them knew what was happening, they kissed. Harry couldn't believe his luck, but then Mary Jane suddenly pulled away.

"I'm sorry," she said. "I should go. It's been lovely, but I didn't mean for you to think—"

"What am I *supposed* to think? How am I supposed to *feel*?" said Harry. He was angry. "You're thinking about Peter, aren't you?"

"I guess I am," she whispered. "I'm sorry, Harry." She grabbed her coat and walked quickly from the room.

"Don't go, Mary Jane!" Harry screamed.

"Please! Don't leave me alone!" But she was gone.

Harry felt like a fool. Like Peter, Mary Jane had stomped on his feelings. There was no reason to take pity on either of them.

His father had been right all along.

Left alone, Harry paced the mansion, confused by the sudden rush of feelings and memories with Mary Jane. He glanced up at his father's portrait, and Norman Osborn's steely gaze met his. Suddenly, he had another flash of memory—a vision of Spider-Man carrying his father's body.

Harry shook it off. He turned, and a mirrored door across the room caught his eye. In it, he saw his father!

"You've taken your eye off the ball, Harry," the reflection said. Harry reached out to touch the mirror, and when his fingers made contact more memories exploded in his brain. He saw himself unmasking Spider-Man! He saw—he *felt!*—his head hitting the ground during his battle with Peter! He saw Peter at the hospital—

pretending to be his friend!

Harry held his head in agony. Opening his eyes, he still saw Norman in the mirror.

"Remember me?" the reflection asked. Harry looked straight into the mirror.

"I remember *everything*," he said.

"Then why haven't you killed Peter Parker?" Norman demanded.

"Things are different now," Harry said. "Peter and Mary Jane are my friends. If I hurt him—I hurt her. And I care about her."

"You have no *friends*," Norman hissed. "She's Peter's girl. He took her away from you. He took *me* away from you."

"I won't listen to you anymore!" shouted Harry. "I have a chance at my own life. Let me be!" Harry meant every word. He wouldn't be ruled by his father's wishes anymore. He stared into the mirror . . . and soon, Norman's face was replaced by Harry's own reflection. He had won the battle. For now.

CHAPTER

8

Harry was surprised when the doorbell rang again later that night. It was Peter.

"Hey, Harry," he said. "I know it's late, but I was hoping to talk to a friend. I've been having problems with M.J. She seems so sad lately."

Despite Harry's earlier victory against his father's voice, hearing Peter talk about M.J. once again stirred up the rage inside him.

"Oh, I don't know. She seemed happy when she was here earlier. We had dinner, we had a play reading. . . . She even kissed me."

Startled, Peter quickly looked up. There was a cruel smile on Harry's face, and Peter knew in an instant what had happened: Harry's memory—and his hatred for Peter—had returned!

Harry was enjoying this. They would battle again, and this time, the New Goblin—this time, the *Osborns*—would win!

"I love her, Peter," said Harry in a low voice. "You stole her from me."

"We both know this isn't really about Mary Jane," Peter said. "It's about you and me. Spider-Man and the New Goblin."

"You stole my father from me and the entire time you pretended to be my friend!" shouted Harry. He leaped at Peter, swinging a super-powered fist!

Peter easily avoided the attack and launched his own, tackling Harry and sending them both smashing through the mirrored door into the goblin lair. Peter was shocked and amazed at the sight of all the goblin weapons. While Peter was distracted, Harry took the opportunity to gut-punch him!

Peter quickly recovered, and his flaring anger fueled his attack. He hit Harry over and over, bringing him to the ground. Despite his strength, Harry was no match for Peter's spider-enhanced abilities. Harry looked him in the eye.

"Are you going to kill me like you killed my father?" he asked.

Peter hesitated. "Your father was a monster and you know it!" he said. "He tried to stab me in the back. I jumped out of the way. He got what was meant for me. And why are you so eager to avenge him, anyway? He never loved you."

"That's a *lie*!" screamed Harry. *"My father loved me!"*

"He despised you," hissed Peter. "You were an *embarrassment* to him!"

Harry was so enraged by Peter's taunt that he broke free and ran to a nearby rack of pumpkin bombs! He grabbed one and hurled it at Peter! Without thinking, Peter created a net out of his webbing and caught the bomb in it—then sent it flying back! The bomb exploded in Harry's face and filled the room with thick smoke.

Screaming in pain, Harry spotted himself in the shattered door-mirror and recoiled in horror at what he saw. Half of his face was completely disfigured.

Peter stared in shock at what he'd done.

"Harry! I'm sorry! Let me help you," said Peter, as he stepped toward him.

"Get out!" Harry screamed. "I never want to see you again!"

Peter did leave. And Norman's voice was silent. Harry could hear only his own sobs as he lay on the floor in pain.

CHAPTER

9

The next morning, Harry lay in his bed. The television was on, but he was in too much pain to pay attention. At least, not until an emergency newscast popped up.

"All of New York holds its breath," a newscaster said, "as the hostage situation continues to unfold." Harry looked at the screen. The hostage was trapped in a taxi that was suspended, in a network of thick black spider-like webs, from the upper stories of a partially completed skyscraper.

The hostage was Mary Jane.

Harry stared at the television. The newscaster continued, "The superpowered villains Venom and Sandman are the ones holding the young woman hostage. Their only demand is that Spider-Man surrender himself to them."

"You're real popular, Pete," whispered Harry to himself.

"I know," said a voice, startling Harry. He turned to see Peter in his Spider-Man suit, standing in the doorway. Peter flinched when he saw Harry's face. The side where the bomb had exploded was hideous and mangled.

"Each of those guys alone nearly killed me in the past," Peter continued. "I can't beat them both. Not by myself." Peter looked him in the eye.

"I need your help, Harry."

Harry turned away from him. Spider-Man had killed his father and had just nearly killed him. Peter wanted his help? Too bad. That ship had sailed.

"You want Mary Jane?" he said. "Well, now you have her. Get out."

Without another word, Peter put his mask on. He walked to the balcony, shot out a web-line to a building across the street, and swung off, heading for all-but-certain doom. He would deal with Harry later—if he survived Venom and Sandman!

Harry buried his head in his hands.

"You're doing the right thing," he heard Norman's voice say. "They both deserve to die. You know that." Harry agreed. But then, why was he so anxious? He stood up and began pacing the room. Soon, he became aware of someone watching him.

It was Bernard. "We must talk," said the butler. "About the night your father died. And about Spider-Man."

"I know all I need to know about that night *and* about Spider-Man," said Harry. "I regret only that I'm not there to help finish him."

Bernard would not be put off.

"The night your father died, I cleaned his wound. The blade that pierced his body came from his own glider. It was his own invention—and only *he* could have controlled it."

"What are you saying?" demanded Harry.

"I am saying," continued Bernard in soft, even tones, "that your father *died by his own hand*."

Could it be true? Harry had known Bernard his

entire life. The butler had always been loyal to the Osborns. But Peter was sneaky and smart. What if he had threatened to kill Bernard if the butler didn't say what he ordered him to?

A few minutes later, a familiar roar was heard as the New Goblin's Sky-Stick zoomed out of the Osborn mansion. Aboard the small craft was Harry, dressed in full New Goblin armor. His loud, chilling laugh echoed through the concrete canyons of Manhattan.

CHAPTER
10

"Why do they always come after *me*?" Mary Jane asked herself. "Do I have the word *bait* stamped on my forehead?" She knew it was a strange time to be joking—but it was the only way she could keep herself from being overcome by panic.

It had all happened so fast. One minute she was in a cab, going to Peter's to try to straighten things out with him. The next, the cab driver revealed himself to be Venom in disguise, and brought her here to lure Spider-Man to his death. It wasn't the first time a supervillain had used her as bait.

They were at a huge construction site. Venom had strung up a vast web over the bare steel girders of an unfinished building. The taxi, with Mary Jane inside it, was snared in the middle, just like the proverbial fly in a spider's web.

Mary Jane hoped Peter would come, and she also hoped he wouldn't. She wanted to be rescued, but she knew he wouldn't stand a chance alone against the two scary, powerful supervillains. Suddenly, she heard a *snap*—and the black webbing supporting the cab tore. The car dropped toward certain doom.

And then it suddenly *stopped* falling!

Spider-Man's webbing had saved her! He swung over to Mary Jane and landed atop the taxi.

"Peter," she said, "they're never going to let you out of here alive."

"We'll see," said Spider-Man, hoping he sounded more confident than he felt.

"The lady's right," said Venom, as he swung onto a nearby girder. A regular guy named Eddie Brock had merged with a strange, alien organism to become this monstrous, spider-like being that had vast strength and the ability to create webbing like Spider-Man. But Venom's web was black and oozing. And Venom hated Spider-Man.

"I'm here. Let her go," said Spider-Man.

Venom suddenly leaped up, kicking Spider-Man in the face, knocking him off the cab.

"Oh, we'll let her go," said Venom, "*after* she watches us destroy you!"

Spider-Man fell ten stories, landing in another section of Venom's elaborate web. Before Spider-Man could get his balance, Venom was on him. They exchanged shattering blows. As they fought, pieces of the web's structure were weakened by the fury of their battle. At last, one key section tore—and the fighters fell toward the ground of the construction site. They hit the ground hard, and for a few seconds, neither one moved.

Spider-Man was the first to get to his feet. He walked toward Venom. "Okay, pal," Peter said. "Once I web you up, I can get M.J. and get out of—"

Wham!

Peter's speech was cut short by the impact of a huge, rocky fist.

"Did ya forget there are *two* of us?" asked Sandman, pleased with his sneak attack. He was an ex-con named Flint Marko, who had been caught in a science experiment gone wrong. It had transformed him into a sand-like substance that he could use in many deadly forms. The force of his sandstone-punch sent Spider-Man stumbling back toward Venom—who had recovered and now smashed Peter with a savage blow of his own!

Spider-Man tried to fire a web to get away, but another sandblast stopped him from doing so. The two villains punched him back and forth between them like a rag doll. They were really enjoying themselves.

Above, part of the webbing holding Mary Jane's taxi in place snapped from the weight of the car. The taxi shifted, and she fell from its open door, grabbing hold of the steering wheel at the last possible instant. She dangled by one hand, sixty stories above the ground.

Seeing this, Spider-Man forced himself to

shake off the effects of Venom and Sandman's attacks. He leaped to his feet and headed toward her. But before he got more than a couple of steps, Sandman sucked up all the sand from the ground and transformed himself into a giant sand-creature. He took off after Peter, nearly crushing him with blow after blow from his giant sandstone fists. Even with his amazing spider-speed, Peter was barely able to avoid them. Sandman then changed tactics, transforming himself into giant sand-hands that could cover more area. Spider-Man fired a web-line and leaped over the huge hands—directly into a powerful kick from Venom! Its impact sent the wall-crawler flying straight back into a girder!

High above them, Mary Jane could no longer hold on. She fell, tearing through layers of weakened webbing until she was able to grab a stronger strand. She was grateful for her good luck . . . until she looked up and saw that the cab—*directly above her*—was tearing loose from its webbing!

Spider-Man was helpless to do anything to save her. Venom had webbed all four of Peter's limbs to a girder and had even wrapped a web-line around his *neck*. Peter couldn't move! He couldn't *breathe*!

One hundred yards away, the New Goblin's Sky-Stick roared toward the scene. Under the mask, Harry's face was still in agony from the effects of the exploding pumpkin bomb Peter had tossed at him. He'd be scarred forever, thanks to Peter.

Harry now held an identical bomb in his hand as he surveyed the scene. He saw Mary Jane about to be crushed. He saw Peter at the mercy of Venom and Sandman. He thought about what Bernard had told him. He thought about what his father's voice had said.

"*Now*, Sandman!" shouted Venom. "Kill him *now*!" Flint Marko had made himself into a sand-giant. He towered over Spider-Man.

"This is it, Harry," he said to himself. "Time

to uphold the honor of the Osborn name!" He aimed the Sky-Stick and flew as fast as he could toward the scene of battle.

Mary Jane saw him coming and closed her eyes. She didn't want to know whose side he would take.